Photo: Archives of *La Presse*.

ANTONIO BARICHIEVICH

BORN 1925, ZAGREB, CROATIA
· DIED 2003, MONTREAL, CANADA

For my father, who is the strongest man in the world.

Editorial Director & Designer: FRANÇOISE MOULY

Translation: RICHARD KUTNER

Lettering and Production: GENEVIEVE BORMES

ELISE GRAVEL'S artwork was drawn and colored digitally.

A TOON Book™ © 2016 RAW Junior, LLC, 27 Greene Street, New York, NY 10013. Original text and illustrations from *Le Grand Antonio* © 2014 Elise Gravel and Les Éditions de la Pastèque. Translation, ancillary material and TOON Books® adaptation © 2016 RAW Junior, LLC. No part of this book may be used or reproduced in any manner whatsoever without written permission except in the case of brief quotations embodied in critical articles and reviews. TOON Books®, TOON Graphics™, LITTLE LIT® and TOON Into Reading™ are trademarks of RAW Junior, LLC. All rights reserved. All our books are Smyth Sewn (the highest library-quality binding available) and printed with soy-based inks on acid-free woodfree paper harvested from responsible sources. Library of Congress Cataloging-in-Publication Data: Names: Gravel, Elise, author. Title: The great Antonio / by Elise Gravel. Description: New York : TOON Books, an imprint of RAW Junior, LLC, [2016] "A TOON Book." Identifiers: LCCN 2016003371 ISBN 9781943145089 (hardcover) Subjects: LCSH: Barichievich, Antonio, 1925-2003–Juvenile literature. | Weight lifters–Canada–Biography. | Strong men–Canada–Biography. | Actors–Canada–Biography. Classification: LCC GV545.52.B37 G73 2017 | DDC 796.41092--dc23 LC record available at http://lccn.loc.gov/2016003371 Printed in China by C&C Offset Printing Co., Ltd. Distributed to the trade by Consortium Book Sales and Distribution, Inc.; orders (800) 283-3572; orderentry@perseusbooks.com; www.cbsd.com.

ISBN: 978-1-943145-08-9 (hardcover)

16 17 18 19 20 21 C&C 10 9 8 7 6 5 4 3 2 1

www.TOON-BOOKS.com

THE GREAT
Antonio

A TOON BOOK BY

ELISE GRAVEL

We don't know much about Antonio Barichievich.

He came from Europe. His dad may have been a woodcutter. One thing we do know is...

...that he was a

VERY big BABY.

Here he is at twelve years old in Croatia, where he was born.

LOOK, NO HANDS!

Little is known about his childhood.
Maybe his parents were

lumberjacks.

Or maybe, just maybe, he came from
another planet where he was raised by

BEARS.

At age twenty, Antonio came to Canada by boat.

He was

HUGE

and very, very strong.

He was six foot three.

Antonio's
CLOTHES

1 HIS SHIRT

You could cut a parachute out of it.

2 HIS SHOES

A large cat could sleep in one of them.

TRUE, BUT BOY, DO THEY SMELL!

3 HIS PANTS

Two mini-Antonios could fit inside.

Here he is, eating.
He could devour twenty-five whole chickens at one sitting
and then down a glass of milk and a dozen donuts if he was
still a little bit

hungry.

He weighed

POUNDS

which is as heavy as a

Here are some more things Antonio liked:

getting dressed up in a tuxedo...

singing arias from Italian opera...

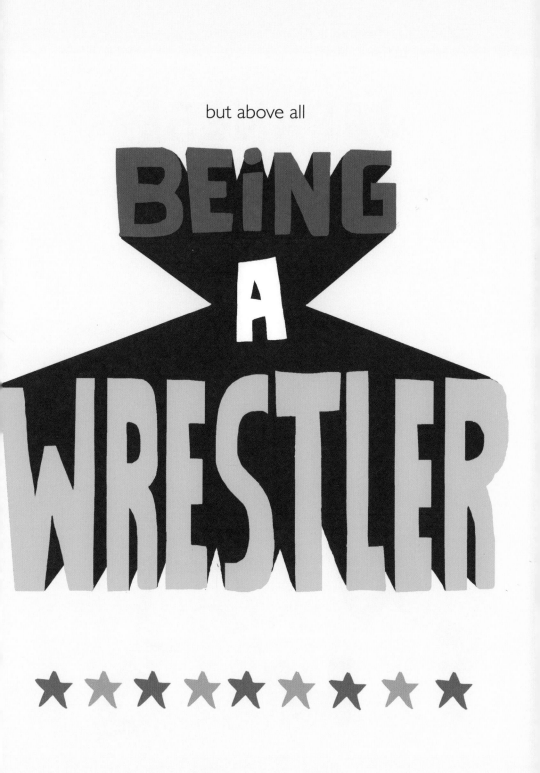

but above all

BEiNG A WRESTLER

Antonio wrestled all over the world.
He fought against...

JAPANESE CHAMPiONS...

against **10** other wrestlers at a time...

...and once even against a bear!

DONG!

He became known in Montreal as "the Great Antonio."
He loved showing off how strong he was. Here, he's
lifting a dozen men hanging on a telephone pole.

THIS IS EASY!

Here, he's pulling a four-hundred-and-forty-three-ton train over a distance of sixty-five feet!

And here, he's dragging four buses filled with passengers.

The Great Antonio loved to pull buses so much that he sometimes pulled them with his

HAIR...

...which he wore in two braids as thick as your arm.
They dragged ON THE GROUND.

Antonio

did all kinds of things

with his

He put pieces of metal inside
his braids and turned them into...

golf clubs...

a cane...

and enormous antennas.

It may be that he used his antennas to communicate with aliens...
and they gave him his strength.

The Great Antonio loved children as much as they loved him.
He twirled them in the air on his braids,
turning himself into a gigantic

**human
merry-go-round!**

Antonio didn't live like everyone else. He liked to sleep

ON THE FLOOR.

He never liked beds—maybe he was afraid of breaking them.

He had a love affair and was sad when it ended.
He stopped spending time at home. From that
point on, he lived mostly on the street.

His office was in a donut shop.
It was the only place he could be reached.

When he died, people placed a mountain of flowers on his favorite bench at the donut shop.

Antonio was the strongest man on 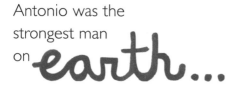 earth...

ABOUT THE AUTHOR

ONE OF MY FAVORITE AUTHORS IS ROALD DAHL. HE GOT ME INTERESTED IN UNUSUAL PEOPLE AND ANIMALS. I'M ATTRACTED TO ANYONE WHO IS STRANGE OR FUNNY.

IN MY HOMETOWN OF MONTREAL, EVERYONE KNEW AND LOVED ANTONIO, THE GENTLE GIANT WHO LIVED OUTSIDE THE DONUT SHOP. HE WAS A GREAT PERFORMER AND SHOWMAN WHO CLAIMED TO BE THE STRONGEST MAN IN THE WORLD.

AFTER HIS DEATH, IT WAS REVEALED THAT MANY OF ANTONIO'S WILD STORIES WERE TRUE!

HE HAD A LETTER FROM PRESIDENT BILL CLINTON AND PHOTOS OF HIMSELF WITH CELEBRITIES LIKE THE SINGER LIZA MINNELLI, THE ACTRESS SOPHIA LOREN, AND THE TALK SHOW HOST JOHNNY CARSON.

TIPS FOR PARENTS AND TEACHERS:
HOW TO READ
COMICS WITH KIDS

Kids **love** comics! They are naturally drawn to the details in the pictures, which make them want to read the words. Comics beg for repeated readings and let both emerging and reluctant readers enjoy complex stories with a rich vocabulary. But since comics have their own grammar, here are a few tips for reading them with kids:

GUIDE YOUNG READERS: Use your finger to show your place in the text, but keep it at the bottom of the speaking character so it doesn't hide the very important facial expressions.

HAM IT UP! Think of the comic book story as a play, and don't hesitate to read with expression and intonation. Assign parts or get kids to supply the sound

LET T   rds so
emerg   zzles,
comic   ence's
under   't be
surpri   u).

TALK   y with
pause   iscuss
how t

ABO   read,
so ga   en in
their   you
won'   ooks,
and

W   M